DINOSAUR Disasters

WITHDRAWN

Kate Agnew  Anna Jones

Green Bananas

EGMONT

We bring stories to life

First published in Great Britain 2010
by Egmont UK Ltd
239 Kensington High Street, London W8 6SA
Text copyright © Kate Agnew 2010
Illustrations copyright © Anna Jones 2010
The author and illustrator have asserted their moral rights.
ISBN 978 1 4052 4778 8
10 9 8 7 6 5 4 3 2 1
A CIP catalogue record for this title is available from the British Library.
Printed in Singapore.

DINOSAUR
Museum

DINOSAUR
Soup

DINOSAUR
Disasters

For Oliver and William,

Darcy and Bonnie.

K.A.

For Audrey and John.

A.J.

DINOSAUR
Museum

It was hot in the museum and very,

very busy.

6

Rosa kept shouting, very loudly.

7

Sam was getting fed up.

'Let's go and see the T-Rex,'

he begged Dad.

Dad was having a bit of trouble with
the buggy.

'Mmm,' he said, trying not to bump
into the triceratops.

Sam knew where to go.

He squeezed in past the man with the

camera and the noisy big girls.

But T-Rex wasn't roaring today.

Something must have

gone wrong.

Dad, Dad!

Sam ran back to get Dad.

Dad wasn't at
the triceratops
any more.

And he wasn't back

at T-Rex either.

Sam was starting to get worried.

He sat down near T-Rex and tried not

to cry.

'Are you lost?' asked a man in a museum uniform.

'No,' said Sam.

Hello there.

'But I think my dad and my baby sister might be.'

'You'd better tell me about them,' said the man.

Sam whispered in his ear.

'Ah,' said the man. 'I know just where

to look.'

And he led Sam round the corner to the

dinosaur eggs.

'Quack,' said Rosa.

'Quack indeed,' said Dad. 'I was

just coming to find you.'

Dad looked at the man and then

he looked at his watch.

'Oops,' he said. 'Sorry.'

The man winked at Sam.

'That's all right,' he said. 'At least it wasn't a real dinosaur disaster.'

DINOSAUR
Soup

Sam was still feeling a bit shaky so

Dad took them to the café.

He said Sam could do some colouring

while they ate their lunch.

Sam got the crayons and the dinosaur

pictures out of his backpack.

Sam ate his sandwiches and
coloured the triceratops blue,
the stegosaurus green and the T-Rex
red like Dad's soup.

Rosa just scribbled, but Dad said that
was fine, she was
only little.

Dad was trying on the explorer hat

from Sam's backpack.

'What colour shall I do the diplodocus?' Sam asked Dad, who was busy testing out the binoculars.

Purple or orange?

'Hocus pocus, here comes

a diplodocus,' said Dad.

He leaned over the table and peered at

Sam's colouring.

'Watch out, Dad!' said Sam.

'The string's going in your soup!'

Dad sat up quickly. His hat wobbled.

Look out!

The soupy string dangled in front of

his top.

'Dad!' warned Sam.

The hat wobbled some more.

Dad reached up to take it off

and the wobbling got

even worse.

The hat slipped off Dad's head,
bumped on the binoculars and landed
– splash! – in the soup bowl.

Oh no!

'Oh bother!' said Dad as he tried to get

the soup off his top.

'Oh dear,' said Dad when he looked at Sam's picture. 'Sorry,' he said.

'That's OK, Dad,' said Sam, trying
not to laugh. 'Red is quite a good
colour for all the dinosaurs.'

'Quack,' agreed Rosa.

Quack!

DINOSAUR
Disasters

Back at home, they made dinosaur biscuits for tea.

Sam stuck some raisins in for
eyes and carefully put his
T-Rex biscuit on the
tray with the others.

They didn't look too good.
The stegosaurus had gone all lopsided
and Rosa's diplodocus looked a bit
like a squidgy snake.

'I think my triceratops is more of an elephant-osaurus,' Dad joked.

'Dad,' said Sam, 'it's not funny.

These biscuits look like

more dinosaur

disasters to me.'

'Don't worry,' Dad promised.

'They'll be fine when they're cooked.'

Twenty minutes later Dad got them

out the oven.

Only Sam's T-Rex still looked OK.

'Never mind,' said Dad. 'Mum will love

them anyway.'

Buster the dog munched the

stegosaurus that landed on the floor.

Rosa woke up crying after her nap.

'Quick,' called
Dad from the
kitchen. 'Give her a
biscuit to cheer her up.'

Quick!

Sam couldn't help noticing that the elephant-osaurus had gone.

He looked at Dad, who brushed a few crumbs off his T-shirt.

'Just checking them,' he told Sam.

Carefully Sam climbed on the stool,

got down a plate and put his T-Rex

biscuit on it.

He took it to his bedroom to wait till

Mum got home.

44

'How was your dinosaur day, darlings?' she called out as she put down her bags.

'A bit of a disaster really,' Dad

confessed, wiping supper off his apron.

Sam held out the plate.

His T-Rex really did look rather good,

Sam thought.

'Yum,' said Mum, taking a bite. 'Now that's what I call dinosaur-delicious.'

Fantastic!

And she gave Sam and Rosa and Dad

a great big dinosaur hug.

'Quack,' said Rosa.

The End.